Marjorie Kendall

NOOGAMICH and other stories

NOOGAMICH
and other stories

Marjorie Kendall

illustrations by
Peter Bjerkelund

NIMBUS
PUBLISHING

Nimbus Publishing Limited
P.O. Box 9301, Station A
Halifax, N.S.
B3K 5N5

Design Editor: Kathy Kaulbach
Project Editor: Alexa Thompson

Nimbus Publishing Limited gratefully acknowledges the support of the Maritime Council of Premiers and the Department of Communications.

Canadian Cataloguing in Publication Data

Kendall, Marjorie, 1930-

A visit from Noogamich, and other stories

(New waves)

ISBN 0-921054-34-3

I. Bjerkelund, Peter.   II. Title.   III. Series.

PS8571.E62V57 1990   jC813'.54   C90-097643-8
PZ7.K46Vi 1990

Printed and bound in Canada

Contents

Preface ix

A Visit from Noogamich 1

The Ticket Home 22

Amy 40

Preface

The great American poet Carl Sandburg once wrote: "There is only one child in the world and the child's name is All Children."

This story is written for all children. It is especially for the defenceless—those children who, like the young Micmac girl in this story, are sometimes laughed at and made to cry or run away. It is for the child who doesn't know where to find comfort, and so dreams about, or imagines a gentle friend—an angel or a grandmother. The friend is someone the child can talk to or feel comforted by.

It is not surprising that the *Noogamich*, or grandmother, in this story is a spirit, for the Micmac people believe that all natural things about them have spirits. They call them "persons." Each "person" is created by the Sun, from whom all things receive life. And these "persons" do not die, but can transcend into other living forms.

When a relative or a very close friend dies, the Micmac believe that the person's spirit may stay nearby, to watch over loved ones. If a child, like the one in this story, needs special help, the spirit of the loved one who has died may come back to offer comfort. It may seem very real—someone you can touch or hug—but it is still a spirit that can come and go in the whisper of the wind, like a dream that seems real when you are asleep but is gone when you awake.

In this tale, a little girl who is very unhappy, is visited by the spirit of her grandmother, *Noogamich*. From the gentle story *Noogamich* tells her, the young girl finds renewed courage.

A Visit from Noogamich

Ten-year-old Kachina Nevin behaved like other young persons her age. She went to school, learned what they did, played the same games. She wore the same kinds of clothes and brought the same lunches.

But she didn't look the same.

Her schoolmates had grey, blue or pale-brown eyes. Hers were dark, almost black. So was her hair. Everyone else had hair of every shade of yellow or brown. Hers was as black as night and as straight as a pencil. There wasn't a curl, a wave, or a crinkle in it anywhere.

Her skin was darker than theirs—a toasty brown.

When she was smaller, these differences in

her appearance didn't seem to matter. But as she grew older, they did.

Boys made fun of her; girls stuck out their tongues.

Not all, but some did.

From those who did, she ran. Clutching her schoolbag in both arms, she hurried through hallways, out of the door, and down the steps.

Kachina lived with her parents and two younger brothers in a house about four kilometres from Rexton, a small town in New Brunswick. Like most students in rural areas, she was driven to and from school in a bus.

"I'm not going back to that school any more," she told her mother one day.

"Why not?" her mother asked.

"Because."

Kachina flung her bookbag into a corner by the steps and ran into her bedroom. The door behind her slammed shut. A drawing that she had tacked on the inside of the door popped loose and sailed to the floor.

Still wearing her jacket and shoes, she

flopped across her bed and jammed her head under a pillow.

Her face felt hot. Tears burned her eyes.

"I don't want to be different." She pummelled her fists under the pillow. "I don't want to be different."

Her mother, who stood by the stove just then stirring something in a pot, couldn't follow Kachina into her bedroom.

Someone else did, though.

Knuckles rapped softly on Kachina's bedroom door. With her head buried, Kachina couldn't hear. The knuckles rapped again, a little louder.

"*Moojeech*." The Micmac word for "grandchild" filtered like warm honey through the wooden door.

A muffled "what?" rose from under Kachina's pillow.

"It's *Noogamich*, your grandmother. May I come in?"

The doorknob turned. The door sighed open.

Drapes were drawn across the windows. The

room was half-dark and smelled musty.

Kachina usually picked up her clothes and made her bed when she came home from school. But this day, she hadn't. The fringed corners of her bedspread dragged on the floor and were twisted together with soiled jeans, a cotton T-shirt, and one ragged-laced sneaker.

The figure of a tall woman in a long skirt whispered across the carpet toward Kachina's bed. As the woman reached the bed, she turned sideways and sat down on the edge. Her weight slanted the mattress, making Kachina roll toward her.

"Oh, *Noogamich*," she sobbed into her grandmother's hip.

The palm of a hand began smoothing her hair. Fingers traced the outside ridge of her ear.

"There ... there," a shadowy, soft voice murmured.

"What's the matter, *Moojeech*?" the voice gently teased. "Did a *buoin*, an evil spirit, crawl up your nose?"

Instead of answering right away, Kachina

pushed herself up with her arms and turned her head. A few long strands of hair hung in front of her eyes. She blew them away. Her grandmother lived in Shubenacadie, and she hadn't seen her for a long time.

"Wh … when … did you come, *Noogamich?*" she asked, her eyes staring with surprise. "I thought you were … you were …"

"Sssh." Her grandmother crossed two fingers over Kachina's lips. "No one knows I have come."

Noogamich was wearing a traditional Micmac dress. This one, earth-brown in color, was laced at the neck, belted with a sash, and was full-skirted to the floor. The sleeves were long and loose. Tribal symbols of life and good medicine decorated the neck, belt, and cuffs of the dress. The same symbols, made with threads of yellow, red, black, and white, were sewn on the square, brown cap that framed her face like an open hood. Her long, black hair was braided into two double strands that looped below her cap. Thin, pink-and-yellow ribbons were woven into the braids.

Native women wear this dress on very special occasions only—at feasts and gatherings.

Kachina wondered why her grandmother was wearing it now, but she was too filled with her own misery to ask.

Her black eyes crinkled shut and her tiny mouth twisted into the shape of a broken heart.

"They laugh at me," she said, and dropped as stiff as a board back on the bed. "All they do is laugh."

"Who are they?" *Noogamich's* hand touched her shoulder, patted it gently, then slid down to rub her back. Kachina felt some of the stiffness leave her body.

"Kids at school. And they call me names … names like redskin and stupid Indian.

"Am I a stupid Indian, *Noogamich?*" she asked, her hands hiding her bowed head. "Am I?"

Noogamich drew in a long breath. The front of her dress swelled, then emptied with a sigh. Her bottom lip was fatter than the top one; she sucked it up under her teeth and chewed at it, as though thinking. Her eyes, half-closed like a sleepy deer's, studied Kachina's bowed head.

How often had she heard her children and grandchildren ask this same question? And how many times had she gathered them to her to tell the story, as she would begin telling Kachina now?

"Come, *Moojeech*." She held wide her arms. A blue-and-white seashell bracelet rattled on her left wrist. "Lean against me, and I will tell you a story."

Kachina snuggled into her grandmother's bulky, warm side and rested her cheek against one soft breast. She felt as though a veil of comfort had settled around her. Her hot face and burning eyes began to cool.

A smell of sweet grass rose from the dress.

Outside the bedroom, her mother was singing and sometimes whistling as she worked.

She heard her father's truck drive into the yard. The sounds seemed far away ... far, far away.

"Once, a long time ago," *Noogamich* began her story, "when the earth hung like a giant, grey rock in the sky, and no person, moose or fish lived on it, there was the sun and there was the moon."

Under Kachina's ear, her grandmother's heart thumped as softly as a distant drumbeat. Her voice hummed through the cloth like bees in a meadow.

"The sun, which was called *Nichekaminou*, and sometimes *S'esas*, became father to us all," her voice hummed on. "High as he was in the heavens, he saw the earth was empty and so filled her womb with seeds."

"Her womb?" Kachina interrupted, raising her head a little as though to hear better.

"Yes," *Noogamich*'s voice chuckled like a brook, "in her womb."

"Oh."

Kachina rested her cheek and ear as before. Her grandmother's hands and fingers played with her hair. Her scalp and neck tingled with good feeling. She snuggled closer.

"Although the seeds he planted all came from

the same bag, each was different," *Noogamich* continued her story. "When he had finished planting the seeds he warmed them with his long, golden arms. Soon they began to grow. The first seeds grew into plants and trees. The second ones grew into animals. The third grew into people."

"Were they people like us, Grandma? Were they Micmacs?" Kachina asked without moving.

"Yes, *Moojeech*, people like us. And everyone else, too," she hurried to say.

"The moon, which we know as *Tepkanuset*," she went on, "became our guardian mother."

"She watched over the seeds at night when *Nichekaminou* was gone," Kachina said.

"Ummm, you could say that," her grandmother answered. "She cried over the ones that were lost, or didn't grow. The tears she shed watered the ones that did grow."

Noogamich made herself more comfortable by leaning her head against the wall and lifting her moccasined feet up to rest on the blankets.

"Now," she began speaking again, "above the

sun and the moon lived the greatest creator, *Manitou*. He was father to all—to the sun, the moon, and everything growing on the earth."

"*Manitou*," Kachina's mouth echoed, "or *God?*" she asked.

"Or God." *Noogamich*'s hood bobbed in agreement. Her looped braids slid up and down the front of her shoulders.

"But," she said, "people growing on other parts of the earth, separated by oceans and mountains, didn't all look the same. Like flowers in a garden, each was made to look different. Some were very fair. Others were dark. And yet others were somewhere in-between. No one had a choice. That's the way we grew. And you, *Moojeech*, with your black, black eyes and black, shiny hair, were made to look very beautiful."

Kachina's eyes grew as round as sunglasses. "Me, Grandma? Beautiful?"

Her grandmother hugged her and went on. "People didn't speak the same languages, either. Everyone called this great creator by different names—names like *Dieu*, *Gud*, *Gott*,

God, Dio, Allah, and many others I don't know. We who grew into *Elnu,* or the first people planted on this side of the earth, began to use the word *Manitou.*"

"Now we say two names—*Manitou* and God. Don't we, Grandma?"

"Yes, *Moojeech.*" Her grandmother smiled. "We say two names."

"Does that mean we know and understand something more than other people?" Kachina asked curiously.

"Well ... ask yourself," her grandmother replied. "Do your schoolmates also think of God as *Manitou?*"

"I don't think so," Kachina frowned, thinking.

"There, you see?" *Noogamich* grinned. A narrow, black slit showed between her teeth. "Doesn't that tiny knowledge make you feel a little bit fuller? A little bit better?

"You can use both names. Most other people have only one."

"I'll bet the kids at school don't know that,"

Kachina remarked as a grin wrinkled her lips.

"I'll bet they don't know what it's like to sleep under the stars, either," she said, thinking of the times in summer when Micmac families gathered by a campfire to share food and stories, long into the night.

She thought some more.

"They don't know much about us at all, do they, Grandma?"

"No." *Noogamich's* reply was heavy with sadness. "They cannot know what they have never been told."

"But what am I supposed to do when they call me names, Grandma?"

"Ah, *Moojeech*." her grandmother squeezed her shoulders and kissed the top of her head. "Only those who don't know any better will do that. And when they do," she rested her chin on Kachina's hair, "you must feel sadder for them than for yourself. And always … always remember.…" These last words she said very slowly and carefully so Kachina might never forget. "You know something they don't. And knowing something always makes you feel fuller and better. Always."

"But ... do I still have to go to school?" Kachina asked in a small voice.

"School," *Noogamich* answered, "is where a person goes to learn things, isn't it?"

"I can learn from you, Grandma," Kachina said.

"But I don't know everything, *Moojeech*," *Noogamich* reminded her. "When I was a little girl like you, I didn't learn to read or write. I can't operate a computer, or fly an airplane—all the things some people do these days ..." Her voice began drifting, as though carried by a summer wind.

Kachina closed her eyes trying to imagine her grandmother flying an airplane or sitting in front of a computer screen. She couldn't.

Could she see herself? She closed her eyes tighter. In the darkness behind her eyelids, forms began to take shape, talk, and move. There was the Micmac lady she saw reading the news on television; Buffy Ste. Marie singing on a stage; her Aunt Cathy teaching in a classroom; her mother, Donna, talking at a meeting. Then another image formed. Was that she? All grown up, going somewhere and carrying a briefcase? What was she? A doctor? A lawyer? A singer? A teacher? A nurse?

Oh …

She began to feel her small self fill and float, as if in a dream. She was drifting, lighter, happier. Her bed carried her like a cloud.

The smell of fish frying brought her back to earth.

Something inside her stomach began pecking like a crow: she was hungry.

Her nose itched. Her hand, sliding up to scratch it, touched something that rattled. A blue-and-white shell bracelet slid down the pillow to rest in the hollow of her neck. It tickled cool. She laced it between her fingers, smiling.

Her bedroom door swung slowly open.

"Hey, Sleepyhead," her father's voice called. "Come and have your supper."

Wasting no time, she scrambled to her feet

and ran into the kitchen.

Only her mother, father, and brothers sat at the table.

"Well! You're looking better now," her mother said with a grin.

"Thanks to *Noogamich*," Kachina replied. "Where is she?"

"Where's who?" her father asked.

"*Noogamich*," Kachina said, sitting down at the table.

Her brothers looked at her as if she had two heads.

"Which *Noogamich?*" her father asked, around a bite of bread. "Your mother's mother from Big Cove, or my mother from Shuben-acadie?" And he winked at her.

"Oh, Daddy," Kachina shook her head at him. "You know. She's here."

"Who's here?" her mother laughed.

"Mother!" Kachina pleaded.

"Eat your supper," her mother said. "Your potatoes are getting cold. So is your fish."

"But she is here!" Kachina insisted. "She left me her bracelet. Look." And she waved the little circle of blue-and-white shells so all could see.

Her mother and father stopped chewing. They knew who had once owned the bracelet. Both stared at it, and at each other.

Her father swallowed.

The bracelet had belonged to his mother, *Noogamich*, who had died three years ago.

"Well?" Kachina asked when her mother and father didn't reply.

"Ah yes, well …" began her father, "Ah, ahem …"

They all knew that the spirits of people who

had died remained always near their families. Sometimes their voices could be heard—in the sigh of the wind, in the trickle of water, or in the call of a bird. And now and then they would reappear in the form of a person, a plant or an animal. But never before had anyone who had returned been known to leave anything behind.

Kachina, who from the time she had been a baby had attended many feasts with her parents in honor of the dead, also knew that the spirits could return. Maybe she had forgotten. Now she was reminded.

"But the bracelet?" she asked. Then, without waiting for an answer, she grinned. "I must be someone very special to *Noogamich*, eh, Mom, eh, Dad?"

Her father, who had been buttering a slice of bread, reached out with his knife and dabbed a dot of butter on the end of her nose. "Very, very special," he said, and smiled.

Her mother's cheeks dimpled. "I don't know what happened to you in your bedroom, or who you saw," she said. "But whatever it was, you seem happier now than when you came home from school."

"Oh, I am, Mom." Kachina's black eyes shone. "I am." And she scooped a forkful of potato into her mouth.

Beside her plate, the little blue-and-white shell bracelet glowed like a warm pearl.

The Ticket Home

Pook Latham and Poke McGuire crouched beneath the bridge. Still as shadows, they watched.

The old Chatham place on the hill above them loomed wide and grey. Moss grew like caterpillars across the straight-peaked roof, and the two tall chimneys bracketed to its sides were capped with bird nests. No one had lived there for a long time. Occasionally, people drove up in cars to look at the house. Some even stayed for a week or two. But no one lived there permanently: no one, that is, except Pook and Poke—and they had no choice.

Poke, taller and leaner, looked over Pook.

"What's happening up there?" His words, slurpy as the stream behind him, floated over

Pook's shoulder. "Who are all those people? And what are they doing?"

Pook didn't answer. He didn't know, so he kept staring.

It wasn't as if the watchers hadn't seen people before. They had—but never so many, and never all at once.

"Why, they are like ants," Pook thought, "in doors and out." One climbed a ladder to the roof. Men and women carrying crates and lamps and potted plants streamed from the far side of a large truck to the pillared veranda, stacked their loads, and turned back to the truck for more.

Another man, watched by Pook, was struggling to free a faded "For Sale" sign from the grip of a thorny blackberry bush beneath a roadside mailbox.

"Let go, will you?" the man argued with the bush.

Hands reached out from inside the house to fling open shuttered windows that creaked when they swung and banged where they stopped. One shutter rattled down from an upper-floor window. Someone shouted, "Look out below!" Ragged curtains billowed outward, and through them a head looked down to make certain no one stood beneath the window. The head weaved from side to side and then slipped inside. The curtains were left hanging outside the window.

"Those people must be moving into the house," Pook finally answered Poke.

"Oh, they are, are they?" Poke murmured ominously.

"Do you see any kids?" he asked, stretching higher over Pook's head in order to see better. "I hate kids. Do you see any?" he asked again.

"Don't think so," Pook replied.

Neither Pook nor Poke cared much for kids. And for good reason, they supposed. The last young person with whom they had come in contact had knocked them clear out of this world, but not quite into the next.

Pook had been a carpenter at the Chatham place then. Actually, he had built the house. Late one evening, as he was sawing lumber by the hay barn some distance from the house, a young boy ran into the barn and accidentally elbowed a burning lamp into the hay. Too frightened by what he had done to even holler, the boy fled through a back door.

Flames crackled behind him. Cows bawled. Horses squealed and kicked their stalls.

Hearing them, Pook dropped his saw and ran into the barn. While trying to set the animals free, he was kicked by a horse and fell unconscious against a wall. Poke, who was the Chatham smith and looked after the harnesses and horseshoes, was asleep in the tack room at the back of the barn. He didn't realize what had happened.

He never wakened.

Before anyone in the house could help, the barn exploded into a raging ball of fire.

All the cows and most of the horses ran wildly into the night, but Pook and Poke were never seen again.

Their spirits, though, remained behind— trapped, trapped on the earth by the careless actions of a boy who didn't even yell out a warning. So they had to wait until another boy

came along who would prove to be more responsible.

He must be someone who didn't run from something that threatened others, but went for help. Only such a boy or girl could free them and let them go home where they belonged, instead of being caught in a world in which they could no longer live.

Not too long after the accident, the Chatham family moved away. The house sat empty. Other people moved in from time to time. If they brought children, Pook and Poke let them stay for awhile. If there were no children, Poke with his icy-cold fingers, scared them away. He would trail all ten of his fingers up their bare legs and arms when they were lying in beds or sitting quietly in chairs. Sometimes, he would drape a sheet around his invisible form and fly around their heads until they ran outside and refused to come back in. All Pook did was moan and wail while tapping a make-believe hammer on ceilings and walls.

Lately, however, Poke was tired of scaring people. He had grown impatient. Of all the young people who had come, not one had acted responsibly. The children had left a gate open so the chickens ran onto the road, had forgotten to turn off taps in the bathroom so water ran all over the floor, or had dropped their roller skates and bicycles where people tripped over them. Poke had begun to dislike all children.

"Rotten kids," he would grumble.

"You had better change your thinking," Pook warned. "One of them might be our ticket home."

Just then a bare-chested, short-legged boy in

flowery, blue shorts and a white, cotton cap ran
from around the corner of the truck.

An older boy with longer legs, the same
flowery, blue shorts, but a green top and cap,
chased him.

"Put your shirt on, Benjie," the second boy
called, waving something yellow over his head.

"Catch me if you can, Dan!" the one named
Benjie sang out, then galloped down the dirt
road toward the bridge.

Pook and Poke crouched deeper in the
shadows. Feet thundered overhead; then they

heard, "Gotcha!" and the sound of scuffling. Dust sprinkled down on their heads. Pook almost sneezed.

"Mom said to put this shirt on, so ... put it on," a determined voice said above the scuffling.

"I'm supposed to be responsible for you while Mom and Dad are busy, so you just do what I tell you."

At the word "responsible," Pook looked at Poke, and Poke looked back.

"Do you suppose ..." Though Pook left words unsaid, Poke knew what he meant.

"We could try," he said.

"Tonight?" Pook asked.

"Tonight," Poke agreed.

The sounds on the bridge above ceased. The boys were running back up the hill toward the house. Benjie, his yellow shirt flapping open, zigzagged in front of his brother, making faces.

"Watch where you're going, Nutsy," Dan warned. "You're gonna fall down and break your face."

The big boy cared! Pook and Poke grinned.

Later that night, when the truck and moving people had gone, the two spirits slipped through a half-opened window and into the house.

Wooden crates and cardboard boxes filled the rooms and barricaded the halls, but where were the people? They searched through all the bedrooms on the second and third floors. No one was there, either.

Then they heard snores coming from the living room. And there, on the old soft carpet, lay the whole family—father, a mother, the two brothers seen earlier, and an older sister. All were wrapped in blankets and sound asleep.

"They'll never hear, nor even feel us," Pook told Poke. "Let's come back tomorrow night; maybe they'll be awake."

Poke looked disappointed, but agreed. "One night more than the thousands we've already spent here won't matter," he grumbled. "I can wait."

The next night fell amid crashes of thunder. Lightning forked the sky, and the old house trembled.

Pook and Poke, however, were already inside and about to work for what they called "their ticket to the next world."

Would the people in the house be scared and run outside, or would they stay? And what about the boy called Dan? Would he prove responsible? Would he set Pook and Poke free? Or … Poke shuddered, would he and Pook have to spend another hundred years in this old house scaring people?

They were soon to find out.

Because the rain had cooled the house,

someone had built a fire in the hearth, and the whole family sat drowsing around its warmth. They had been busy all day and were tired. Some sat on the floor. Others reclined on easy chairs and a sofa. The electricity hadn't been connected yet, so two oil lamps burned on a low table in front of the sofa.

Poke began his antics.

The owner of the first bare leg up which he ran his cold fingers looked startled but didn't jump or scream. So Poke tried again. This time he let his fingers linger and pinch a little.

"What the...?" was all that person said, jerking her leg away.

"What's wrong, Chrissie?" the boy called Dan asked. He was sitting cross-legged on the floor next to her chair, and her jerking leg struck his.

"Don't know," she complained, rubbing the spot Poke pinched. "My leg feels cold and sore, all at the same time."

"Probably this drafty, old house," a man said, yawning from some cushions on the sofa.

"Ummm ... ummm," another voice, a

woman's this time, agreed sleepily. She was rubbing the tops of her bare arms with her hands. "I'm feeling cold, too."

Poke moved away from her.

No more was said until a hammering sound began around the room. Wails and moans and groans accompanied the hammering.

"What's that racket?" The woman stopped rubbing her arms to look up. "Must be the wind whistling through an open shutter," she said, then looked down at the boy beside her. "Dan, go upstairs and check all the shutters, will you?"

"Sure, Mom." Dan got to his feet, picked up a lamp, and left the room.

The old house was three storeys high, with many rooms. Dan would be gone for some time.

Knowing he would secure the noisy shutter and silence the wailing wind, the family let themselves relax.

Benjie, youngest and smallest of the five, fell asleep on a rug in front of the fireplace. Chrissie had crawled into a sleeping bag beside him.

Their mother sank deeper into her lounge chair. Everyone's eyes had closed. They were asleep.

The man on the sofa rolled over. One of his feet nudged the lamp burning on the table.

The sleeping man's foot moved again. So did the lamp, sliding closer to the edge of the table. It was tottering!

Pook and Poke stared with horror. There was nothing they could do!

The lamp fell on the carpet with a dull "thud." The glass globe didn't break, but the oil, licked by thirsty flames, spread.

"*Oooowwwwoooo!*" Pook began the loudest longest wail he had ever attempted in all his years of being a spirit. Again and again, he wailed.

Poke, whose cold fingers were of no use now, began to moan.

The sounds carried—out into the hallway and up the first flight of stairs, until they reached Dan at the far end of a hall. They made his hair tickle his head, and he raced down the stairs, yelling as he ran.

At the foot of the stairs, he was stopped by

a bulge of flickering light from the living room.

"Fire!" his mind screamed, then his mouth.

"Mom!"

"Dad!"

"Chrissie!"

"Benjie!"

"Wake up! Fire!"

Grabbing a blanket from a box of bedding in the hall, he covered his head and ran into the flames. He still held the first lamp in one hand. He flung it into the hearth and grabbed Benjie.

Wakened by Dan's screaming, his mother,

father, and sister leaped up and began smothering the flames with more blankets from the hall.

Pook and Poke continued their wild wailing. Then, when the fire was nothing but a reeking mass of smoke, they silently thanked Dan and slipped out of the window the way they had come.

Outside, blending as one with the now-quiet, moonlit night, they let themselves be carried beyond the bridge, up to the stars ... and home.

Amy

My name is Petrie. I remember this old stone house; I used to live here a long time ago. I've come back to fulfil a promise I made many many years ago.

I've been looking around my old home for the past few days, trying to find my way. Things sure have changed. It was always a large, rambling house, but other families have altered its appearance—many times, by the look of it. It's been painted and repaired. New rooms have been added, and others seem to have been torn down. Most of the cave-mouthed fireplaces that once gave warmth on cold Maritime nights have been bricked up. Instead, potted ferns and brass peacock tails hide the hearths, and some strange kind of heat warms all three floors at once. I heard someone call it "central heating." I don't know what kind of heating that is. I've

tried to find out where it comes from, but all I know is that it's all around, sometimes too warm, almost suffocating me.

That was when I opened a window to let in the cool air.

The people who now live in my house became very excited and began to run around in circles.

"Who opened that window?" someone asked. "Did you? Did you?" They looked mystified, and then someone closed it again.

This used to be a mill house. It was here that farmers brought their grain to be ground into flour. There is a narrow river called the Tatamagouche that runs along the far side of the house. Once, the river turned a great wooden wheel that, in turn, caused enormous, round, flat stones inside the building to revolve slowly and grind the grain placed between them.

My grandfather was the captain of a great clipper ship that sailed out of Halifax Harbour. It was he who laid the first stone for the foundations of the house. He also made a widow's walk for his wife, my grandmother. There was a small, railed veranda built on the roof, where she could feel the sea breezes blow up the Tatamagouche and watch for my grandfather's return. It's still there.

My father didn't like the sea, so he decided to become a miller, instead. He built the great wheel.

Yesterday, I went to see if the wheel remains. It does, but it is in a different place now. Someone has hauled it out of the river, reinforced the sides with shiny metal poles, and set flower pots on each great paddle. The grinding stones have been made into picnic tables and stand on a cement patio where cows once grazed. Six chairs made of some kind of curly, white tubing surround the stones. Pink-and-white-striped sunshades blossom like giant flowers from the middle of each table. A flat expanse of lawn, lilac hedges, and flower beds covers a crushed-pebble-and-seashell lane where wagons and carriages were once driven around the house while the milling was being done. There are no horse droppings any more;

we used to call them "road apples."

The house is in the same place, near the widening mouth of the narrow river. But the trees and bushes have grown so tall and thick that the house can hardly be seen from the road. If a large, square sign near the highway didn't have an arrow pointing down the gravelled road toward the river, no one would know it was there at all.

I noticed the sign the day I arrived. Its newly painted words read, "Wheel House Inn—Bed and Breakfast."

"Wheel House Inn," I chuckled to myself. "Wait until I tell my Grandpa Captain."

I noticed many other changes on my arrival, some that still puzzle me. No one lights gas jets any more, or carries lamps or candles up to bed at night. Now there are balls of glass, milky white or yellow, stuck under lamp shades, on walls, or hanging from ceilings. The white ones light up the dark so that every corner of a room can be seen.

I was very curious to know how these balls of light worked, so I watched quietly. One evening, I saw someone pull a switch on a wall, and, immediately, the ball flashed with a blinding light. Of course, I wanted to see if I could make this happen and so I went into many of the rooms, trying all the switches.

This caused even more excitement than the open window.

"What the…? What's happening?" they asked, bumping into each other.

There is another thing I don't understand. In some of the rooms there are small, square boxes with screens. Each box is filled with tiny, puppet-like people who are play-acting. How any one of the boxes can hold so many chattering people and animal puppets is a mystery to me! And, most wonderful of all, the puppets have no strings! They are worked by pushing buttons.

I had a merry time pushing this one and that one, until the real people sitting in front of the boxes looked up with startled faces and jumped off their chairs.

"Who did that?" they demanded, racing forward with fingers extended to press more buttons and turn little wheels. "Someone call a repairman."

After a few days, all these things that I didn't really understand became boring. That was when I rediscovered the room that had always been my favorite—the library.

Except for those light balls, it was the only room in the house that hadn't been changed. No screened boxes chattered from corners. The fireplace was free of ferns or screens; it was laid with paper and wood ready to be burned.

I struck a long, wooden match from a clay jar by the coal hod and lit the paper. After staring at the dancing flames for awhile, I turned away. The smell of books was everywhere, familiar and comfortable. Firelight brightened the gold lettering on their spines. They looked like old friends, warm and welcoming.

I was just about to reach for one when half of the library's double door slid open.

"Oh, someone has lit a fire! How nice!"

I looked, and there, framed in the middle of

the enormous, wood-panelled doorway, stood a little girl. I don't know how old she was. I'm not very good at guessing ages, but I don't think she was any younger than me when I was alive. She was pretty, though. Her hair hung like a veil around her shoulders. It was dark and long and parted in the middle. A pale, heart-shaped face glowed softly in the firelight, and her searching eyes were as grey as the foggy sea. She wore a print flannelette gown with ruffles that touched the tip of thick, white socks. On her feet were fluffy, green slippers.

I knew immediately that she was the special person I had been sent to meet, but I didn't want to move in case I knocked something over and frightened her away. So I just stood, watching.

The girl shut the door quietly and walked slowly toward the fireplace. For awhile, she stood looking down into the flames. Her hands were folded loosely in front of her, and she swayed from left to right as though listening to some unheard melody. I think she was smiling.

On the bottom shelves that lined the walls were children's books. Turning her back to the fire, she made her way across the room, bent over, and studied their titles.

"Which one shall I read tonight, Corky?"

Corky? I looked quickly about.

We were alone in the library.

"Which one … hmmmmm … hmmm? Which one?" she was singing to herself.

"How about *Winnie the Pooh?*" she asked, turning toward an easy chair and talking to a rag doll in a calico dress. The doll, with its flat, freckled face and yellow-wool hair peeking out from a floppy hat, didn't answer, though I half-suspected it might.

"That must be Corky," I thought, still not moving.

With the book in one hand, the little girl pulled a lamp chain with the other, then sat in the deep arm chair and held the doll on her lap.

She opened the book and started to read out loud.

Fascinated by the story, I forgot all about the book I was reaching for and sat down on the worn, but soft, carpet to listen.

As she neared the middle of the story, she began to yawn. In a short while the book slid off her knees. She seemed to be asleep.

Cherry-pink, fat-tongued embers were smouldering in the fireplace when I heard, "Hello. Who are you?"

"Why ... Why...." I scrambled up from the carpet, surprised. "I'm Petrie."

"Hello, Petrie. I'm Amy."

She held out her hand as though to shake mine, which we did, but didn't, if you know what I mean.

My mouth formed a large "O." She seemed even prettier, with a soft light that glowed from within her—like the first rays of a morning sun, or the halo around a candle flame.

"I've never seen you before," she said, looking me all over. "Do you come here often?"

"No. But I hope to now that you're here," I told her.

"Do you come here often?" I asked her in turn.

"Only sometimes." And she looked back at

the figure of herself in the chair.

"My parents don't like me to sit too long in this old library. It's dusty and bad for my health, they say."

"Why?" I asked.

"I've got something wrong with my body; it's called leukemia, so I'm not very strong."

"Leukemia?" I wondered, never having heard the word before. "Where is it?"

"In my body, over there on the chair." She nodded over her shoulder. "It's a disease that weakens my blood," she added—much as if she was talking about the weather or the furniture. "They say I won't live very long."

I didn't know how to answer, so I said nothing.

"Have you travelled much?" She changed the subject.

"Yes, in a way," I told her.

"I've travelled," she admitted shyly.

"Have you?"

"Oh yes," she replied. "I've been to wondrous places." She clasped her hands together. "Only," and here she seemed sad, "whenever I tell anyone, they don't believe me."

"Why not?" I wondered out loud.

"They say I make it all up." She looked down at her gown. "They say I dream things."

"And do you?" I, who had never before lived in two worlds at the same time as she seemed to do, was totally mystified.

"Well," she replied, "you tell me. Is this a dream?"

"I don't think so." I shook my head.

"There, you see?

"I can't travel too far yet, though." She changed the subject again.

"Oh?" I was very curious. "Why not?"

"Because I have to return to my body all the time."

"Oh." Now I really didn't know what to say.

"But I'm here now!" Her eyes brightened. "And I'd like to go somewhere!"

"How do you usually go?" I asked cautiously.

"It's easy!" She laughed. "I just open a book! Would you like to come with me?"

How could I refuse so wonderful an invitation?

So we debated what book to enter and, because she had said she couldn't go far, we chose *Anne of Green Gables*. That would take us just across the Northumberland Strait to Prince Edward Island.

But before we were even able to open the cover …

"Amy," someone called. "Amy?" A taller child, with long blonde hair, entered the library. "Why you naughty girl!"

I recognized the speaker as her older sister, Jenny. I had seen her before about the house.

"Here you are again. And you've lit a fire in the fireplace—breathing in all that smoke. Oh, what am I going to tell Mother? Wake up, Amy."

The girl bent over and tapped Amy's arm where it rested across the doll. "Wake up."

"I've got to go, Petrie," Amy told me hurriedly. "I've got to go. But I'll be back. Wait for me … wait."

And like a deeply drawn breath, she was sucked back into her body on the chair.

Wakening, Amy rubbed her eyes, looked up

at her sister, and then at where I stood.

"I suppose you were dreaming again," Jenny said to her not unkindly.

"Yes." Amy sat up eagerly. "Oh, Jenny, I met this friend. His name is Petrie. We got along so well together. And … and …"

"There, there," Jenny murmured, smoothing her younger sister's long, tangled hair. "It's okay, Pumpkin. I'll take you up to bed."

Using both arms, she helped her sister up from the deep chair and, tugging down on the lamp chain, turned off the light ball.

"Goodbye, Petrie." I saw Amy's pink lips form the words over her shoulder as she was carried slowly out of the door. "Goodbye."

Amy seemed much weaker in her own body than out of it, as though she were very, very tired.

I never get tired so, though the night was black, I slipped through an open window and up to the widow's walk to look around. I tried to be careful and not kick things over, but I did anyway. A loose shingle here, a cracked chimney pot there, went crashing down to the deck below. (Cats are always able to see me, and a couple that did leaped off into the darkness, their tails in the air as stiff as the fur standing on their arched backs.) Windows below were banged open. Heads were poked out.

"What's going on up there?" voices yelled to the rooftop.

Skinny light tubes beamed upwards, piercing the night. One of the tubes flashed across a flying cat.

"Oh. It's those darned cats again."

Lights went out. Heads were pulled in. Windows were slammed shut—such a commotion. I kept very quiet then until morning, when there would be enough light in the library to read.

Amy didn't come to the library the next day or the following one. Nor did I find her in any of the rooms when I went looking.

Finally, I heard her mother say sadly to someone who asked that Amy was in a hospital.

"The poor dear," that someone answered.

"Will she be home soon?"

"Tomorrow," Amy's mother replied. "She's coming home tomorrow. She'll have to stay in bed, though," she added, touching the corner of her eyes with a handkerchief. "She's not very strong."

I hurried to the library, gathered together some books that I thought Amy might like to travel through while she rested in bed, and carried them up to her room. Then I sat down on a footstool to wait.

"Did you bring those books up here, Jenny?"

"Me?" Jenny looked at the stack of books I had dumped on the bed.

"No." She shook her head thoughtfully, a look of wonderment filling her face. "No, I didn't."

"Someone else must have, then. Please take them back downstairs. Amy will be too tired to read when she comes home."

The mother's face looked pained, as if she was hurt deep inside herself.

"Yes, Mother." Jenny spoke quietly.

"I wish they hadn't done that," I thought. "I

know Amy would like to read."

After Jenny returned the books to the library, I waited until no one was around. Then I carried some upstairs again. Only this time I brought just two books, and Corky the rag doll.

"Well, for goodness sake!" Amy's mother exclaimed nervously. "Jenny! What's going on? Didn't you take those books back downstairs?

"And how did that dusty old doll get up here?"

Jenny put her arms around her mother's shaking shoulders.

"Hush, Mother," she whispered, as she held her. "Hush. Maybe Amy is meant to have the books. That's why they keep coming back."

Her voice was soft, almost a whisper, but her intelligent eyes looked a little scared. I wished I could put my hand out to stroke the worry lines from her forehead.

"The books can't hurt her now, Mother," Jenny said.

"Yes, but she dreams things," her mother fretted. "And when she dreams, she doesn't rest. And if she doesn't rest, she'll get weaker.

And … oh …" The older woman sobbed into her hands.

Jenny's eyes studied every light and shadow in the room. I could tell she was looking for me. I could hear her thinking, "Petrie? Petrie?" Amy must have told her about me.

But I didn't answer. She wouldn't have heard.

The next morning, I found Amy in bed in her room. She was sleeping. Her hair fanned out across the pillow like dark waves on a pale beach; her face looked tiny, almost the same color as the pillow.

I looked down at Amy and wondered about the leukemia that was making Amy ill. Perhaps it was like the influenza that had separated me from my body that winter I fell off a boat and into the icy water.

I tried to remember the feeling, but it was all so long ago that I couldn't.

I did recall what happened when I was released, though, and I wanted to tell Amy's mother and sister so they wouldn't worry so much, or be so afraid. I wanted them to know that I was here to help Amy.

It took place in this very room, only there were a lot of people standing around my bed. Their faces were sad and they whispered to one another. My eyes were closed but I could see and hear, because I wasn't in my body. No, I sat on a tall clothes closet with my knees drawn up under my chin, looking down at everyone. I wore a long, white cotton nightgown and socks, and I sat as quiet as a cloud. I felt neither happy nor unhappy; I just watched.

Then someone, I don't know who, but a pleasant, gentle someone, led me away. And as we went she whispered to me, "One day, you may be asked to help another child find her way. You must promise to help."

And I did.

Then we entered a huge domed building, like a cathedral without seats, where we milled around with a lot of other people—figures waiting. There were small beings and tall ones, shrouded and veiled. We talked, but without words. No one rushed. There was no hurry. The light was dim, I remember. We seemed to be waiting for something to begin.

Then a great pair of doors swung slowly inward, and everyone turned toward them. One by one, we floated toward a soft light that glowed at the end of a long, dark corridor. Some of the figures turned around to move back the way we entered. They seemed sad but said nothing.

The light before us grew rounder and rounder until we seemed to be walking right into the gold-silver face of a full harvest moon. And once inside … oh, the wonder! There were trees, but the leaves and blossoms were unlike any I'd ever seen. They looked like bubbles of spun glass and reflected a million colors, like diamonds in the sun. Rivers flowed silver water. Flowers sparkled like jewels. Everything shone. Even the shapes of buildings radiated living light. And the figures around me smiled with wonder, as I did.

Amy stirred beneath her blankets. I returned from my reverie, looked down at her, and recalled the promise I had made to that special person who had helped lead me from my body so long ago. I was glad I had been chosen to come back to help her.

Amy reached for Corky. The doll had slid onto the floor. I bent down to pick it up when,

"Hello, Petrie!" Amy stood beside me and took the doll in her arms. Her face glowed even more than before.

"You brought me some books!" She smiled happily. "There's *Heidi* and, oh, *Anne of Green Gables!*"

She danced around, hugging the book and the doll to the front of her nightie.

"Let's read, Petrie." She handed me one. "Let's go somewhere."

I took the book.

Her bedroom door opened.

"Oh, you're awake, Amy! How nice. How are you feeling, sweetheart?"

It was Amy's mother bending over her figure, brushing her hair back from her brow, touching her face, kissing her cheek.

"The doctor's here to see you, love."

But Amy just stood beside me. The doll and books were on the carpet where she had dropped them when the door opened.

"Amy!" Her mother's voice grew sharp. *"Amy!"*

She turned to run out of the door, bumping into someone coming in.

"Doctor! Doctor! She's not breathing … she's not …"

A dark-suited man brushed quickly by her to Amy's side. His fingers moved in a blur. His hands slapped her chest, pumped her body. Taking a long glass needle from his bag, he injected it into her, just below her heart.

Amy was whisked back into her body again. But not before whispering to me one faint word: "Wait."

On the bed, her chest started to rise and fall. Her eyes opened, and she smiled weakly at her mother. Suddenly, her eyes flashed brighter, wider, as though she were staring at something over and around her mother's head.

"It's so beautiful, Mother," she said, her face lit like a small sun, "so very, very beautiful." And she reached out her arms toward her.

Amy slept most of the time after that. She

didn't come out of herself to visit me much, and when she did, it was not for long. The doctor had given her medication to rest and to ease the pain. Jenny or her mother sat beside the bed or tiptoed quietly so as not to wake her.

When Amy did open her eyes, they looked so sad. Tears filled their corners and slid down her thin face onto the pillow. Some rested like dewdrops in her hair.

I wanted to help, but I couldn't.

Amy knew I was there, though, for when she looked my way, she smiled. She saw me all the time now without needing to leave her body.

I didn't go away from the room any more. I was worried she might miss me and have no one to guide her when she left her body forever.

And then one day, much as it had happened to me, Amy left her body for the last time. Like a sigh, she wafted upward to the top of the clothes closet where I sat with my knees tucked under my chin … waiting.